For Sara, who told me of the White Fox, and for all those who feel out of place in the world

First published in 2016 in Great Britain by
Barrington Stoke Ltd, 18 Walker Street, Edinburgh, EH3 7LP

This paperback edition published in 2017

www.barringtonstoke.co.uk

Text © 2016 Jackie Morris
Illustrations © 2016 Jackie Morris

A CIP catalogue record for this book is available from the British
Library upon request

ISBN: 978-1-78112-739-1

Printed in China by Leo

The White Fox

JACKIE MORRIS

Conkers

1

>•<

The day the fox came, things began to change for Sol.

It was a white fox, a wild thing, alone in the city, lost, just like him. That's what Sol had thought when his father came home from work and told him about the fox as they ate a late supper together.

Just like him, except he wasn't completely alone. He had his father. But his father was always busy.

He never had time for Sol, didn't make time to understand him.

"At first the guys thought it was a cat, one of those feral creatures that act as if they own the docks at night," his father said. "Then one of them saw it clear in the security lights, prowling in and out of shadows. An Arctic fox, large as life and twice as beautiful, living alone on the dockside. Amazing."

Sol tried to imagine the wild white fox stalking along the docks, feeding on scraps left by the dockers, on mice and on rats.

"Where do you think it came from?" he asked his dad.

"Who knows?" his dad said with a shrug. "Escaped from the zoo? It's a mystery for sure. Did you get a card from your gran today?"

"Yes." Regular as clockwork, Sol would get a postcard, a letter, on the same day every week, from Gran, from 'home'.

He passed this week's card to his father.

"Funny," he said, turning it over in his hands. The card showed a bold Inuit drawing of an Arctic fox. He smiled at the coincidence. "Can I read it?"

Sol reached across, took the card from his father. He scanned the words, written in a formal, masculine hand. He wanted to read his gran's words himself.

"She says she hopes we are well, asks about school, says she has a birthday present for me, something we should go visit to pick up. Doesn't say what it is. Then it's all a bit confused. And she says Grandpa's finding it harder to go fishing on his own, so come. But they are OK."

Sol's dad stared out of the window. It seemed he had stopped listening a while back.

"So, what can I get you for your birthday?" he asked his son.

Sol just shrugged. He knew what he wanted, but he was too scared to ask. He'd learned that disappointment hurt.

"What will they do about it do you think?" he asked instead.

"What?" His father didn't have a clue what Sol was talking about now.

"The fox. What will the dockers do about it?"

"Don't know." Sol's dad shrugged back at his son. "Guess they'll have to catch it somehow. Can't have an Arctic fox running wild in the city."

Sol wolfed down the rest of his supper, grabbed the card from the table and took a long hard look at the drawing of the fox, then picked up his battered skateboard and headed out.

He just heard his dad call, "Be back before nightfall," then the clattering of dishes being cleared as he slammed the door behind him.

Sol's father stood at the window and watched his son skateboard smoothly down the street.

There was a worried half-smile on his face. His boy was such a loner of a child. He thought how

maybe he should take him to see his grandparents,
so he could go fishing with his grandpa, see how the
old folks were. But going back home was so hard,
since Sol's mother had died. Memories of her were
strongest when he was there. In Seattle he could
lose himself in the noise of city life.

2

Three days it took Sol. Well, three evenings. The days were wasted in school, keeping his head down, hiding from bullies, trying not to let his mind wander away from the endless drone of another dull class.

Evenings, away from school, away from home, Sol wandered among the massed containers of the docks. He was on a mission.

All the dockers were used to seeing him. He often came to work with his dad in the school holidays. But on these evenings he kept out of everyone's way, searched all the dark places where he thought a fox might hide. He found a couple of red foxes, mangy and thin-looking creatures. The place was alive with feral cats, scrawny wild things that hissed and scratched if Sol got too close. But no sign of the Arctic fox.

On the third night Sol sat on the old dock, next to the big crane that loomed like a strange insect above him and tried to imagine how such a creature as the white fox would come to be here.

It was from so far away. From another world. A world where his gran and grandpa lived. A world that Sol longed for in a way that sometimes made him fierce angry with frustration because he couldn't go there as often as he would have liked. Every time he asked, his dad would come up with some excuse.

Sol sat for so long, seeing nothing, that he began to think perhaps the dockers had been mistaken. Maybe it was just a cat that they had glimpsed after all.

The water of the Puget Sound flowed by, a steady dirty brown expanse. All around him was curiously quiet. He was still as stone, lost in his thoughts. And then a movement caught his eye. White in the shadows, running, then still.

A white fox!

Eyes like flames.

Sol watched. He felt the heat rise in his face, his heart beat faster as he focused all his attention on the one small white creature, so strange, so alien, so wild in this landscape. He forgot to breathe. He thought he could scent snow on the city air.

And the fox came closer.

Maybe it recognised in Sol a kindred spirit.

Maybe it hadn't seen him, sitting still like a stone, all alone.

Maybe it thought he was part of the landscape.

Maybe it was needing food, and pure hunger had driven it past fear.

Closer the fox crept, and closer, and Sol slowly reached into his bag and pulled out a peanut butter sandwich.

The fox stopped, stiffened. Wary, swaying gently from paw to paw, unsure. Sol threw the sandwich into the space between them and fast as white lightning the fox darted in, snatched it and ran to the shadows.

Sol let out a long sigh. So, the fox was real. An
Arctic fox, lost amid the Seattle docks, out of place,
all alone, just like him.

3

For three weeks Sol went down to the docks.

Every evening he would be there, drawing the white fox in a little closer, trying to gain its trust. He didn't really have a plan, didn't know what he would do if the fox came to trust him. All he knew was that when he had first seen the fox he had felt his spirits lift, had felt them soar then settle with some connection he couldn't put into words. He felt calm. Pure calm. As if everything – problems with school, with his dad, everything – tumbled away and there was just him and the fox and the two of them was all that was important.

All day Sol would worry about it, afraid the fox would be found and caught. His dad had spoken about it a few times, how the animal welfare people were down the docks trapping the feral cats again. Every now and again they would do this. His dad told him they took the cats to animal shelters where they were re-homed, but Sol wasn't sure. No one

would want these crazy stunted spitting wildcats.

He had his own ideas of what happened to them.

On Wednesday evening everything changed. Sol
was bolting down his supper, grunting answers to
his dad's boring questions about school. Another
card had come from his gran. She said she hoped
he could persuade his dad to bring him for a visit to
fetch his birthday present. If not, she said, surely
he was old enough to travel alone now.

Sol was about to rush out the door when his dad said, "Oh, yeah, remember that fox I told you about?"

Sol froze. He felt sick.

"Yeah?"

"They caught it yesterday."

Sol's heart lurched and tilted with fear.

"You OK, boy? You look pale. Sit down."

Sol sat.

"The fox?" he said.

"Yeah. Some of the boys borrowed one of those humane traps they use for the cats, baited it with a peanut butter sandwich. And bang! They trapped it straight away."

Sol could feel tears behind his eyes, his heart hammering, his fists clenching.

"Want to go and see it?" his dad asked.

Sol nodded. He didn't trust himself to speak.

"Come on then."

4

>•≼

They drove to the docks in his dad's old station
wagon, his dad chattering nonsense like a crazy
bird all the way, but his words made no sense. They
tangled and twisted in Sol's mind as he tried to keep
calm, to think.

It was his fox. His fox. Trapped.

They walked into the office together. Four
dockers sat around drinking dark tea. And there, at

the back, was a small cage filled with a white fox, its startling eyes like bright fire shining out at the room.

"Don't go too close, son," his dad said as Sol moved towards the terror-stricken fox.

Sol fought back the tears, the frustration, the fear. The men chatted, but they seemed almost as agitated as the fox.

Sol inched closer. What had he expected? That he would befriend the fox, tame it? That it would live with him and his dad in their apartment? That he would take it back to its Arctic home? He dropped to his knees in front of the cage and as he did so the creature stopped shivering, pushed its thin body against the bars, then sat and looked at the boy.

The whole room fell silent now.

"Well, would you look at that," his dad said, and Sol turned to see the room full of men watching the boy and the fox. "It's like they know each other."

"What's going to happen to him?" Sol tried to keep the tears from his eyes and the desperation from his voice.

"Well, we're not sure. We called the cat people and they said there was nothing they could do, him not being a cat," one of the dockers said. "They said

call the police, or animal welfare. Welfare said they only deal with pets, so we called the police."

Sol listened, his heart in his mouth with fear.

"At first the police laughed, thought we were playing a joke on them. How did we think an Arctic fox could get from Alaska to Seattle? Then they said they would send a marksman down to shoot him because he's a 'non-native species'."

"No, no, no, they can't ... Dad, you have to stop them." Sol leaped up and grabbed his dad's arm, shaking him. "No, you can't let them." He couldn't remember a time when he had felt so scared and so helpless.

"Hang on, hang on, just a minute now, lad," the docker said. "Listen. Calm down."

Like Sol, the fox was shaking again now, scrabbling at the cage, agitated. The noise of its scratching and ragged breath filled the room.

"No one's going to shoot your fox, boy."

"What do you mean, Sol's fox?" his dad asked.

"Where's your boy been every evening for the past few weeks, Ben?" the docker asked. "That kid's got the patience of a saint."

Ben looked at his boy.

"What do they mean, Sol?"

But Sol couldn't answer. He stood between all of the men and the white fox in its cage, as tall as he could. Tears ran down his face, but he no longer cared.

"No one is going to shoot my fox," he said. Despite the tears and a heart filled with fear, he found that his voice was steady, resolute.

"It's OK, son," one of the men said. "It's OK. There's no way we'll let them shoot him. Here's what happened. Old Charlie told the police to hang on a minute, then he banged some stuff about, picked the phone back up and told them the fox had just escaped, so they could save their bullet. For now your fox is safe. But if we let him go again we'll soon have half the cops in the district down here for target practice. So, what now?"

They all looked at Sol's dad. Sol's dad looked at his boy.

"The fox needs to go home, Dad. Back to Alaska. So do we. You asked me what I wanted for my birthday."

"Wait a minute, son. You can't have a fox for your birthday. He's a wild thing, not a pet."

"No, listen." Sol stood tall, looked his dad in the eyes. "You asked me what I wanted. I want to go home, to see Gran and Grandpa. It's been too long.

And I know I can't have a fox, and it's not yours to give anyway. But he needs to go home. God alone knows how he got here, but he doesn't belong here. He belongs to the wild. Take us home. Please."

5

Sol and his dad bought a bigger cage down at the local pet store, bolted it into the back of the jeep. It took a couple of days to organise time away from work, away from school. Then together they headed north – man, boy and wild white fox.

The journey took six days. In all his 12 years, it was the longest time Sol had spent in the close company of his father.

At first they travelled in awkward silence. Sol had taken a book out of the library before they set off, *Animals and Birds of Alaska*. As they rumbled along the road north, he read aloud from the chapter about the Arctic fox.

"It says that the Arctic fox can live further north than the red fox. Where their territories cross, the red foxes bully the smaller white foxes. But because its size means that it needs more food, the red fox can't survive in lands where the white fox can live."

At night they slept in one of the cheap motels strung along the roadside. They would smuggle the fox into their rooms, feeling like conspirators as they did so. They couldn't let the fox be found, afraid it would be taken from them if it were. Their feelings for the fox, the joy they felt each new night that he was safe, brought father and son closer together.

Sometimes as they drove, Sol would wriggle and scramble into the back of the jeep to check the fox was OK. He would lie beside the cage, reading, and after a while the fox would come over to the bars, curl against them, tail wrapped over his nose, bright eyes watching the boy. Sol would drift off into dreaming, playing with the mystery of how the fox came to be in the docks at Seattle.

By the second day Sol and his dad were talking,

about things that had been silent between them for

years.

"I don't remember her," Sol said.

He didn't need to say who – his dad knew.

"And then sometimes I feel guilty because I

don't remember her. Not her face, her voice, her

smell. Nothing." Sol sighed, his heart sore. "There's

an emptiness where I feel something should be."

"You were only two years old," his dad said.

"When she was hit by the car."

For a while they travelled in silence, then,

"Every day I remember her face, Sol, when I look at

you," his dad told him. "You are so like her. Every day."

The boy looked across at his father's profile as he drove. He thought of the mother he couldn't remember and all the memories his dad must have of her. Looking at his father now, he felt he was seeing him, *really* seeing him for the first time.

"Every day I miss her," his dad went on. "Every day I feel guilty. She never wanted to go to Seattle. It was my fault. I thought we'd have a happier life there. More money, a better job, better school for you."

Sol knew when to be quiet, to let his father speak.

"We grew up together, you know. Childhood sweethearts. My family moved away when I was about your age. After school I went back to find her, terrified that someone else would have won her away from me. The minute we saw each other again we knew."

They pulled over at a roadside diner.

"I'm going to get coffee, you want anything?"

Sol shook his head. All he wanted was time to take in what his dad was saying.

"Check your fox then. I won't be long. I'll phone your gran. Let her know we're coming."

6

That day, as night started to fall, Sol's father asked, "What are you going to call him?"

"Huh?"

"Your fox. What's his name?"

"He's not my fox," Sol said. "He's wild, untamed. He doesn't need a name. At least not one I could give him."

His dad laughed. "She named you just right, boy. Solomon. You've got your mother's wisdom as well as her looks."

Sol thought for a while. "You never talked about Mum before," he said. "And why did you never take me to visit Gran and Grandpa? Apart from for the funeral. And I don't really remember that. Why? Was it too painful?"

"Something like that," his dad replied. "Hard to look your grandparents in the eye, feeling like it was my fault, having taken their daughter away. And the missing her becomes so big when I'm

there, where we grew up, with all those memories of running wild in the woods. Life was easier then, when we were kids."

"But that's not true, is it?" Sol said. "It's just what grown-ups think because they remember all the good bits and forget the rest. It's not easier."

And now his own words began to tumble out.

"Take my life. I hate school. I endure it because I have to. I have no friends. The other kids hate me. Well, no, they don't hate me – they're scared of me, because I look different with my black hair and dark eyes. I think different. They call me

'Shaman Boy', taunt me and say I have the devil in me."

Sol paused for breath, unsure where that had all come from. He'd been dealing with it day to day on his own. But now it was out and couldn't be put back, he was glad. Life wasn't easier when you were a kid. It was just that grown-ups wanted it to be that way.

His dad turned to look at him. "Do you want me to go into school, talk to the Principal?"

"God no," said Sol. He couldn't imagine anything worse.

7

After six days on the road, living in each other's
pockets, father and son had started to get to know
each other a little better. But when they arrived at
Sol's grandparents, they both became a little shy.
The old couple had the wisdom to let them settle,
giving space to man, boy and fox. A table was set
with a simple meal. Gran asked Sol about their

road trip, about the white fox, and they all went out to see how he was.

"Well," said Gran, "there you are now. Look at you. She doesn't seem any the worse for her long journey."

"She!" Ben and Sol chorused.

"Well, yes. Obvious really. She's a vixen. Had to be if you think about it."

Sol looked at his grandmother and smiled. Something about the way she looked back at Sol told him she had a secret. A secret to do with the fox. Sol knew that only patience would draw it out of her. And, by the look she gave him, that secret was all about love.

Sol and his dad had planned to stay for a week, let the fox go, miles from town, then head home.

So, one morning, the four of them set off together into the forest, hoping to make a long day of it, an adventure. When they came to what looked to be a good place they opened the cage door and

walked to a stand of birch trees, not too far away, so they could see what happened.

After a short while the white fox came to the open tailgate, looked around. Docks, cranes and containers were now replaced by tall trees and the soft earth of the forest floor. There was a scent of snow in the air, a covering on the ground. She jumped down and then, without a backward glance, headed off deeper into the trees.

As she went, Sol felt a curious pull towards the wild. His grandmother raised her hand in a salute and he thought he heard her sigh, "Thank you." Just a whisper.

Ben saw them and smiled. How odd that this small fox had brought his family together again.

8

Sol loved his grandparents' place. He loved the ramshackled chaos of it. He loved the space of it. There was a great wide yard, enough rooms to get away into if you wanted to be alone.

The old house was filled with carvings of creatures, in soap stone, serpentine, and found pieces of whale bone and antlers. Bears, black-beaked loons, musk ox, seals, walrus, and of course,

Arctic foxes. When Sol asked where they all came from his gran just smiled and tapped the side of her head.

"Come with me," she said, and she led the way out of the house to a neat little shed.

It had lines of wooden shelves filled with stones and images. A brazier stood in the centre and tools hung from tidy hooks on the walls.

On one of the shelves a photo was propped up. Sol walked across and looked – and saw a woman, young, happy, a sleeping baby strapped to her back. She stood, black and white in the photo, in a stand of birch trees. Sol picked it up and looked for a long time. His mother. And him, when he was a baby. And yes, he did look like her. As he stared at this familiar stranger, his grandmother began to talk.

"Your mother, Sol, was a sculptor. Did your father never tell you? Ah, well, you know now. I taught her first. Well, she watched me when she was a child and later joined in. But her skill far surpassed mine. She went away to college. Some of these are mine, many of them are hers."

"Incredible," Sol gasped. "But why did Dad never say?"

"Well, he couldn't bear to have things around that reminded him of her. All her sculptures that weren't sold came back here."

Sol looked around in wonder, then picked up a mallet. It felt so good in his hand.

"You want to learn?" Gran asked.

Sol's smile told her all she needed to know.

When Sol's dad came to find them he was astonished to see the two of them working away at a piece of white soap stone.

"Be careful with those tools," he said. "They're sharp. You OK him being here?"

"Oh yes," Sol's grandmother answered. "You're never too young to learn. And anyway, it's where he belongs."

And so the one week stretched into two.

Grandmother and grandson worked away at the white stone until he ached in his body and his mind, but the peace he found in the stone was worth the blisters on his hands. She taught him how to see the shape inside the stone, how to take away rock to make it emerge, tap tapping to reveal what was hidden to other eyes, but had always been there. And while they worked they talked.

About stone.

About tools.

About his dad.

About his mum.

About school.

And then about the fox.

"Your mum," his grandmother said, "had a special affinity with the white fox. There was one in the garden on the night she was born. For that matter, it was the same the night you were born, even though you were so far away. She would often see them. She used to dream about them."

"I've been dreaming of white foxes too," Sol said. "Strange dreams, wild white foxes in the sky."

Gran smiled.

"More than anything your mum loved to sculpt them. And her foxes were always what sold first."

She paused. "Anyway, not long ago, a few months maybe, I was settling down to sleep when I heard the bins being knocked over. I thought it would be a big old bear, but when I went out to look it was a hungry white fox. So, I put some food out for her that night and for a few nights after and then one night she was gone."

"Gone where?" Sol asked, wondering where his grandmother's tale would take them.

"Into the forest, I thought. But then a neighbour who works on the garbage boats told me a story. It seems he'd been working on a ship that took the rubbish down from Alaska to Seattle. They would pick up dumpsters, take them down the coast. It seems that on this one trip they'd got to Seattle and there was a stowaway."

Sol put down the tools he was working with, leaned against the stone.

"They'd been hearing strange noises all the way down the coast," his grandmother went on. "But as they neared Seattle they felt sure there was a baby crying in one of the dumpsters. And when they opened the lid what should jump out but a raggedy, half-starved white fox. It ran off into the depths of the ship and they never saw it again. They figured either it had died of starvation or somehow come

ashore in Seattle. Maybe that stowaway was your fox?"

As Sol listened to his grandmother's story a strange idea came to him. "Did you send her, Gran? Is she what you were sending me for my birthday?" Even as he said it he realised how odd it sounded.

"Well, maybe." She smiled. "Or maybe she was your mum, finding a way to bring you and your father home. To remind him of something."

Sol could hear his dad outside, laughing with his grandpa. He tried to remember the last time he had heard him laugh. He couldn't.

9

>•<

Then came the day when it was time to go back to Seattle.

"Let me give you that present now, Sol," his grandmother said. "I'm so glad I didn't have to post it. I would have hated for it to have become lost."

She handed him a box. A plain box, dark and heavy.

"You should have had this years ago," she went on. "It was the last piece she made before she died. No one else has ever seen it. She made it for you."

Sol held the box in his hands.

He'd never had anything that was his mother's before, let alone something she'd made just for him.

He opened the box.

Inside was a beautiful Arctic fox, carved from a piece of antler, decorated with fine detail.

The fox sat in the centre of the table as they ate breakfast together. After breakfast his dad told Sol to go and pack.

"No."

Sol looked at his dad. "I'm not going," he said. "I'm staying here. And you should too. It's where we belong. You know it is."

Sol's grandmother and grandfather stood to clear away the breakfast dishes, and then they found some very interesting things to do in the kitchen, leaving the two to talk.

"We can't just stay, Sol," his father said. "I've got work. You've got school."

"I've told you what I think of school. I hate it. There's a school here."

"You can't just run away from bullies, son. You have to stand up to them. You can't let them drive you away. You have to stand and fight."

"I'm not running away," Sol told him, his voice level. "This is our home, Dad. And it's not my fight. I didn't ask them to pick on me. I don't want to fight them. I don't want anything to do with them. This is my home and I am staying and I hope you will too."

Ben looked at his son. Solomon. He wondered when it was that he had become so wise.

Later that day, Sol's dad drove back to Seattle alone, to sort out the remnants of their life in the city.

And the next morning, Gran took Sol to enrol in the local school. From his very first day there he felt an enormous sense of being at ease, the relief of being among people who had no reason to fight him.

Sol spent his evenings learning to shape stone, how to carve bone into shapes and images and memories. He knew now what he wanted to do when he left school. He would be an artist.

10

>•≼

One evening Sol was sitting by the fire with his
grandparents. He was still reading the huge book
on Arctic animals he had borrowed from the library
in Seattle, learning about the creatures. He got up
to show his gran the book, wanting to point out a
passage about foxes following bears and wolves to
find food. She wouldn't look at the words on the

page and seemed uncomfortable with the book, almost embarrassed to be holding it.

"Sol," his grandpa said, looking up at them both. "Neither your gran nor I can read. We never learned. We never went to school."

"But my cards?" Sol said, not making sense of what he was hearing. "Every week you wrote me cards."

Gran spoke this time.

"I went to a friend who acts as a scribe for those of us who can't read or write. With you both so far away, I needed to keep in touch – somehow. I'd take your replies too and he'd read them to me."

"But why?" Sol asked again. He couldn't understand. Everyone could read, couldn't they?

"It's the way it was for some of our people when we were young. Things happened. Some of us went to school, some didn't. At the time the government would take children away from the People, put them into missionary schools. Teach them basics. Some of the children were adopted and their parents told they had died. Your grandpa and I both came from nomadic peoples. They kept as far away from government as they could and we were raised in the old ways, with the old gods. Some in government thought us lower than animals. They didn't try to understand.

"So, we learned the things school doesn't teach you. We learned how to hunt, how to butcher, how to respect the land, the animals. We could navigate across sparse territories, day or night. And we learned our stories, passed down for centuries. The old ways, that's what we knew. But not reading. Not writing."

Sol thought about all that they knew, had learned. He thought about how much he had learned from books. He thought about how hard it must be to manage in a world where words have

such power. He thought about how he used writing,

even something as simple as making lists to remind

himself of things, and how clever you would need to

be to hold it all in your head without writing. And,

most of all, he thought about all the books he had

read and how he took refuge in stories when life

was hard for him.

Sol took the book from his grandmother's hands

and read the passage about Arctic foxes to her as

they both listened.

For a while they were quiet, then he said,

"Remember what you said to Dad when he first

found me in your studio, when you were teaching me how to sculpt?"

"What?" she asked.

"You said, 'You're never too young to learn.' Well, reading isn't such a difficult thing when you know how to do it. I could teach you. Or you could go to a class at the library and I could help. I would love to teach you. After all, you're never too old to learn a new skill."

For an hour they sat together, Sol and his grandparents. He began by showing them the shape of the alphabet. Its 26 letters. Not so much to learn. They talked about how they fit together,

looked at the shapes of simple words. Sol felt warm inside, knowing he had so much to teach them, excited to know he had so much more to learn from them.

They talked about how they could write down the stories of the People, to keep them safe, so they could be shared. Sol imagined the stories of his grandparents in libraries around the world. It made him smile with a fierce pride.

11

>•<

That night, before Sol went to bed, he stood on the decking outside his new home. Tomorrow his dad would be back with all their things – and the thought of him on the road made Sol realise how much he had missed him.

A glimmer of white moved in the shadows of the dark garden. Sol raised a hand in greeting.

His grandmother came out to stand beside him.

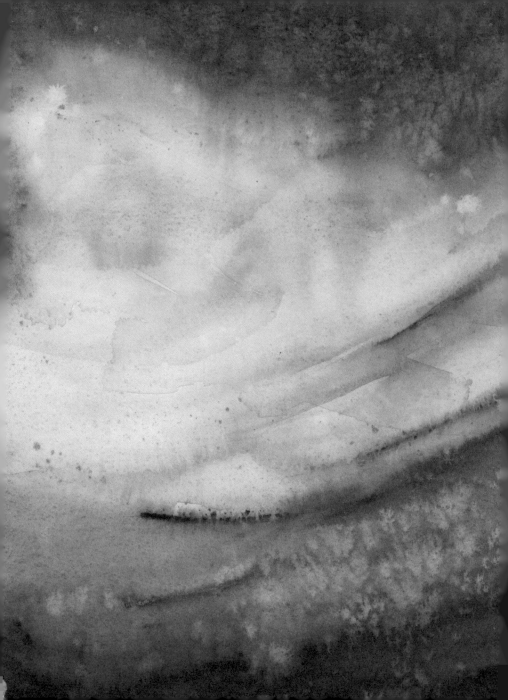

For a while they stood in silence, watched the Northern Lights dance in the sky.

"There are those who say the Lights are made by a great fox running over the snow, brushing her tail in the drifts, sending bright sparks up high," she said. "But the People believe the Lights contain the shadows and spirits of the dead, dancing to remind the living that they are still there, watching over them."

And at the end of the garden, in the shadows, the fire-coloured eyes of a small white vixen watched the boy and his grandmother as they smiled at the dark sky.